Tiberius
and the Friendly Dragon

Keith Harvey
Illustrated by Heather Kirk

Award Publications Limited

ISBN 978-1-84135-917-5

Written by Keith Harvey
Illustrated by Heather Kirk

First published by Tiberius Publishing Limited

This edition first published by Award Publications Limited 2013

Published by Award Publications Limited,
The Old Riding School, The Welbeck Estate,
Worksop, Nottinghamshire, S80 3LR

www.awardpublications.co.uk

13 1

Printed in China

For Lauren and Heather

This is a story about Tiberius, a little white mouse. His ears were pink …

… and his tail was EXTREMELY long.

One sunny morning as he scampered along, he came to a signpost.

One way pointed left.

And the other way pointed right.

Left   Right

'Which way shall I go today?' he thought. 'I'll go left.'
And off he went down the winding path that led into the village.

On the way he met some of his friends.

"Hello!" he called to Ladybird as she nibbled a sweet green dandelion leaf. "You're out and about early today," he said to Bee as she buzzed along the hedgerow.

His friend Snail was still curled up inside his shell house. Tiberius tapped gently. "It's only me, Snail. I think you've overslept this morning. Everybody is out and about except you."

Eventually, Tiberius arrived in the village, and the first thing he spotted was a large notice.

An important meeting to be held in the village hall this morning.

Please come, everyone!

'I wonder what that can be about?' thought Tiberius. 'I'd better go and find out.'

Tiberius was most curious to find out what the meeting was all about, so he crept into a corner and sat very still. After a while a policeman came out onto the stage.

"Good morning, everybody," he said in a loud voice. "Thank you all for coming.

"You must be wondering what this special meeting is all about. Well, I'll tell you. A scary red monster has been seen on the side of the hill."

Everyone in the hall gasped and a few people turned quite pale with fright.

"I am very busy at the moment," said the policeman, "and I would like someone to go and see this red monster."
Everyone went very quiet.

"Sorry, I can't help," said the postman. "I've got so many letters to post."
"I couldn't possibly go," said the milkman. "I've got the milk to deliver."
"Terribly sorry," said Mrs Cake. "I have all the baking to do."
'This is ridiculous,' thought Tiberius. 'Someone must help.'

"I'll go!" he shouted.

"Who said that?" asked the policeman. Everyone looked round to see who had volunteered.

"I'll go!" shouted Tiberius again, scampering up onto a chair. Everybody in the hall began to clap and cheer.

"Right then," said Tiberius. "Where exactly is this large creature?" The policeman gave Tiberius the directions and advised him to be very careful.

Tiberius felt very excited as he walked out of the hall.

He began climbing the hill where the strange red monster was supposed to be.

Halfway up the hill, Tiberius stopped for a rest. He looked down at the village and thought it seemed a long, long way away.

Then he looked up and down the hill and wondered where the strange red creature could be.

He carried on a little further, but still there was no sign of the monster, just some puffs of smoke going up into the air.

'I wonder what that can be,' thought Tiberius. 'I'd better go and investigate.'

He crept on up the hill, when suddenly ...

... there before his very eyes was a big red monster, sitting outside a cave with his head in his hands, puffing out clouds of smoke.

"I know what that is," said Tiberius to himself. "It's a dragon!"

Tiberius decided to walk straight up to him and say hello. But as soon as the dragon saw him he jumped up and ran into the cave.

"Come back!" called Tiberius.

"Go away! Please go away," said the dragon. "You frighten me."

"Me? Frighten you?" said Tiberius, and he started to laugh.

"Whoever heard of a timid dragon?"

"Well, I *am* timid," said the dragon. "And so would you be if you didn't have any friends. Whenever anyone sees me they shout and scream and run away and then that frightens me."

"Oh dear," said Tiberius.
"Don't be frightened. You
must have some friends."
"Well, I haven't," sniffed the
dragon, and he started to cry.
Tears ran down his cheeks,
down his nose,
over his chin,
onto his chest,
and along
his tail.

"Come on," said Tiberius. "I'll be your friend. Let's shake hands."

The dragon slowly put out his hand and Tiberius shook it. "A friend!" shouted the dragon. "I've got a friend!" And he began to smile.

"What shall I call you, little mouse with pink ears and an extremely long tail?"

"Call me Tiberius," said the mouse.

"And I will call you Drag."

Tiberius thought for a moment.

"Do you know something, Drag?" he said. "I've always wanted to be big like you."

"And do you know something, Tiberius?" said Drag. "I've always wanted to be brave like you."

They chatted and chatted together until it began to get dark.

"I'd better be going back to the village," said Tiberius. "Will you come back again another day?" asked Drag. "Of course I will," said Tiberius. "I'm your friend now."

When Tiberius got back to the village everyone was waiting for him.

"Are you all right, Tiberius?" they asked. "You've been away for a long time."

"I'm absolutely fine," said Tiberius. "In fact, I've had a very special day. I've made a new friend and one day I'll bring him to the village to meet you."

"Yes, yes," said the policeman anxiously,
"but did you find the scary red monster?"

"Oh yes," said Tiberius. "He is my new friend!"